Patch the Perfect Kitten

"Oh Louise," her mum said, briskly. "Don't look at me like that. You know we can't keep Patch. If we kept all the kittens that got handed in to us we'd have hundreds by now!"

"But I don't want to keep *all* the kittens," Louise murmured. "I just want to keep Patch!" She couldn't explain why Patch was special to her. He just was.

All of Jenny Dale's KITTEN TALES books can be ordered at your local bookshop or are available by post from Book Service by Post (tel: 01624 675137)

Patch the Perfect Kitten

by Jenny Dale

Illustrated by Susan Hellard

A Working Partners Book

MACMILLAN CHILDREN'S BOOKS

Special thanks to Gwyneth Rees

To Magnus and Hattie, and in memory of
Matilda – three perfect cats.

First published 2000 by Macmillan Children's Books
a division of Macmillan Publishers Limited
25 Eccleston Place, London SW1W 9NF
Basingstoke and Oxford
www.macmillan.co.uk

Associated companies throughout the world

Created by Working Partners Limited
London W6 0QT

ISBN 0 330 37456 7

1 3 5 7 9 8 6 4 2

A CIP catalogue record for this book is available from
the British Library.

Typeset by SX Composing DTP, Rayleigh, Essex
Printed and bound in Great Britain by Mackays of Chatham plc, Kent

Chapter One

"Let me out!" the kitten miaowed from deep inside a large wet cardboard box. He nosed against the lid to try and open it.

The box had been dumped beside someone's front door, and for the past hour the wind and the rain had been steadily falling on it. The tiny kitten inside was getting very wet, very cold and very frightened. "Help!!!" he yowled again, and this time it was so loud that the box around him shook.

A door opened and a strange voice said, "What was that noise?"

Suddenly the box was opened and a girl's face looked inside.

The kitten trembled and desperately tried to hide in the corner.

"Oh, you poor thing!" said the girl as she took the box inside the house to where her parents were getting everyone's breakfast ready. Twenty bowls of cat food took quite a long time to prepare, so her mum and dad were very busy indeed.

"Now, what have you got there, Louise?" Mrs Dodds, her mother, asked.

"Someone left a kitten outside the front door. It looks *so* cold and frightened!" Louise carefully lifted the tiny bedraggled kitten out of the box and cuddled it close to try and warm it up.

"What a scrawny little mite! It doesn't look very old." Mrs Dodds examined the kitten more closely. "He's a tom, and he looks like he could do with a big breakfast."

Hearing the word *breakfast*, the kitten miaowed hungrily and tried to wriggle out of Louise's

arms to reach the tasty dish of cat
food Mrs Dodds was holding in
her hand.

"Better take him into the clinic
and warm him up first," Louise's
mother said, stroking the little
kitten on the top of his head. "I'll
be there in a minute. I'll bring
some water and some food."

"Oh, Mum! Can't we keep him

here, in the house?" Louise begged.

"Now, Louise! You know the rules! We have to check all newcomers out first before they can mix with the other cats. The vet's coming in this morning, so we can get your new friend seen straight away."

Reluctantly, Louise did as she was told.

As she carried the kitten back out into the hall, he looked up at her for the first time. Two bright green eyes, round and blinking, fixed on her and then the kitten gave a little miaow and started to squirm as the front door loomed closer.

He miaowed, trying to bury his

head in Louise's woolly jumper.

"Don't worry. You'll soon be nice and warm," Louise reassured him, opening another door and carrying him through to the clinic. She gently set the kitten down on the shiny metal table while she went out to fetch a clean blanket.

The kitten, left all on his own, miaowed again sadly.

Another, louder miaow greeted him from a large cage where a plump grey kitten with amber-coloured eyes was curled up, inspecting him. "Don't worry, she'll be back in a minute," the bigger kitten said. "So how did *you* end up here, then? You don't look very well . . ." he yawned, politely. "Still . . . I suppose they must be expecting you to live or they'd be making more of a fuss."

"Of course I'm going to live!" the younger kitten miaowed. *Although if someone doesn't bring me my breakfast soon, I'm not so sure*, he thought. In his last home the people often went out to work

and forgot to feed him in the morning.

"So how *did* you get here, then?" the grey kitten asked again.

"I was left outside this house and a young girl called Louise found me."

"Ooh, you were lucky! *My* last owners tried to drown me but I got rescued. My name's Oscar by the way. This place is all right. They'll find you a new home to go to, that's for sure. I'm leaving just as soon as I've seen the vet."

"The vet?"

"That's right," Oscar said. "He's the man who makes sure you're fit and healthy. He looks a bit fearsome but he's not so bad really. Hey, I'd stop scratching if I were you. They'll think you've got fleas! Maybe you *have* got fleas! Don't come near me if you have, I've just got rid of mine!"

The little kitten started to tremble. He remembered his last home and someone shouting at him:

"*FLEAS*! HE'S FULL OF *FLEAS*! I TOLD YOU WE SHOULDN'T HAVE GOT HIM! HE'S GOING STRAIGHT TO THAT CATS' HOME UP THE ROAD, THAT'S WHERE HE'S GOING!"

The kitten miaowed miserably. He was sure he'd be sent away again just as soon as everyone found out he had fleas. People didn't like fleas, but then kittens didn't like them either. It was horrible to be nipped at all day long and have those horrible itchy pests in your nice coat and not be able to get rid of them.

"Here you are!" Louise called out, coming back into the room with a warm blanket. The little kitten was shivering as she wrapped him in it. "Hey, there's no need to be frightened. I'm not going to let anyone hurt you."

She stroked his head and laughed. "You're going to have a lovely tortoiseshell coat soon. Now, what shall we call you? What do you think, Oscar?" Louise asked the other kitten. "Shall we call him Patch, since he's so patchy all over?"

Oscar blinked his large amber eyes and looked at Patch's scrawny coat. It was so grubby that Oscar didn't see how Louise could tell what colour it was going to be. Oscar twitched his nose in Patch's direction to try and get a sniff of him. Oscar hoped Patch didn't smell as bad as he looked, especially if they were going to put him in the empty run next to his.

"Well Patch seems a reasonable description of him, I suppose," miaowed Oscar to no one in particular.

"Well, I like it!" Patch replied. "It's much better than the name those other people gave me."

As Louise cuddled him, Patch wanted to warn her about the fleas because he didn't want them biting *her*. So he told her about them in the only way he knew how: he reached under his chin with his back paw and scratched at his neck vigorously.

"Oh, dear!" Louise sighed. "We'd better ask the vet to give

you something to get rid of those. Don't worry, soon you won't be itchy at all. You really are a handsome kitten, Patch! We'll find a home for you in no time, and until we do I'm going to look after you myself!" She sat down with Patch on her lap and turned him over on his back so she could tickle his tummy.

Patch had never had his tummy tickled before. And it was a long time since he had made the funny noise he was now making. It was a sound that seemed to be coming from his chest and causing his whole body to tremble. And it was so loud!

"Don't worry!" Oscar called back to him, cheerfully. "You're purring, that's all. It just means you're happy."

Patch realised that he *was* happy. And the more Louise stroked him and talked to him, the happier he felt.

When Louise's mum came in a few minutes later with a big bowl of cat food, Patch felt happier still.

Chapter Two

"I've put some chopped meat on top this morning as a special treat," Mrs Dodds said as she handed Louise a bowl of food to give to Patch.

It was now several days since that first morning when the vet had given him an injection in the scruff of his neck and sprayed nasty-smelling liquid all over him which made his fur tingle. Patch hadn't enjoyed seeing the vet one bit but luckily his fleas hadn't either. They'd all disappeared and hadn't come back since!

No one had ever given him fresh meat to eat before and he had to ask Oscar what it was.

"It's chicken," Oscar said, his nose twitching at the smell of it. "Most cats can't stand it. Bring it over here and I'll eat it for you if you like."

Since the chicken smelled so tasty Patch decided to try a piece anyway. And he was very glad he did! "I *like* chicken!" he miaowed excitedly to Oscar. "I'll be able to eat all *yours* for you now if you like!"

But for some reason, instead of being pleased, Oscar seemed quite huffy and went and lay down with his back to Patch and started to chew his claws. His tail was swishing as if he was cross.

"Oscar, you've already had some chicken this morning!"

Louise laughed, which made Oscar's tail swish even more.

"Louise, there's a young couple with a little boy coming to look for a kitten tonight," Mrs Dodds said, carrying a bucket and mop towards Patch's run. "Why don't you give Patch a good comb when you get home from school? Try and smarten him up a bit?"

Louise didn't reply. Patch noticed she had stopped smiling.

"Oh, Louise," her mum said, briskly. "Don't look at me like that. You know we can't keep Patch. If we kept all the kittens that got handed in to us we'd have hundreds by now!"

"But I don't want to keep *all* the kittens," Louise murmured. "I just want to keep Patch!" She couldn't explain why Patch was special to her. He just was.

But as it happened when the young couple came they walked straight past Patch and picked a white kitten that had come in the day before. Patch was glad to see that kitten go because every time he had tried to be friendly towards her she had just ignored him as if he smelled funny.

The following week, after Louise had gone to school, Patch and Oscar were allowed in the kitchen while Mrs Dodds was cleaning out their runs. Patch had never been in a kitchen before. He thought it looked very exciting.

"Now, no scratching anywhere but here!" Mrs Dodds said, firmly tapping the scratching post as she set it down in one corner.

"Where else would we scratch?" Patch asked, looking round after Mrs Dodds had gone. The kitchen had a wooden floor with no bits of scratchy carpet in sight.

"She means here!" Oscar said, demonstrating how well he could sharpen his claws on one of the big wooden table legs. "And here!" He bounded over to have a go at some bumpy wallpaper next to the fridge. Soon he was so excited that his tail bushed up. He began to race around the kitchen, leaping up onto chairs and down again and into the

litter tray and out, sending litter
flying everywhere as Patch
watched.

Patch wanted to play too. He
was just waggling his bottom
ready to pounce on Oscar when
Oscar leapt up onto the kitchen
table out of reach. As Patch
jumped up to join him, the
kitchen door opened.

"PATCH!" Mrs Dodds shouted,
crossly.

Patch looked down in confusion
at Oscar, who had jumped down
as the door opened and was now
sitting innocently licking one
paw.

"PATCH!" Mrs Dodds yelled
again. "GET DOWN!"

Patch jumped down quickly. He

hated being shouted at. Luckily, at that moment, the doorbell rang and Mrs Dodds went to answer it.

"They don't like cats on the table," Oscar explained. "Next time you'll have to jump down quicker when you see them coming." He straightened his paws out in front of him and gave a long stretch, followed by a yawn. "I hope the house I'm going to live in has a nice warm fire. If it has, I'm going to lie down right in front of it all day long. It's going to be purrr . . . fect!"

"They might not have the fire on all day long!" Patch said, feeling a little sad. He always felt upset when Oscar boasted about his new home, because he knew he didn't *have* a home yet. Well, not one where he could get to stay for ever and ever.

"I hear that old ladies always have their fires on all day long," Oscar said, smugly. "And they give you lots of milk – even though the vet says it's not good for you." Oscar licked his lips at the thought. "I got picked straight away! When it comes to choosing kittens, people always go for the cute ones first."

Just then Louise's mum came back into the room with an elderly lady close behind them.

"Here's your new mum, Oscar," Mrs Dodds said, picking him up.

"Mrs Smith, I don't suppose you want *two* kittens to keep you company, do you? This is Patch and he needs a good home too!"

Patch held his breath because Oscar wasn't looking too pleased. Patch felt pretty sure that Oscar had set his heart on being an only cat.

"Well, aren't you a handsome boy?" Mrs Smith said, smiling at Patch.

"Yes, he is *now*," agreed Mrs Dodds, proudly. "But you should have seen the state he was in when he first arrived!"

Mrs Smith thanked them for offering but said she really could only manage one kitten just the same. So the last that Patch saw of Oscar was a final swish of his grey tail as Mrs Smith popped him into her cat basket. But he couldn't stop thinking about what she had said. *Handsome*, she had called him. No one but Louise had ever called him *that* before!

Chapter Three

Patch felt lonely after Oscar had gone. He cheered up, though, as soon as he heard Louise's voice calling out his name later that afternoon. Louise always came to see him as soon as she got home from school.

"Patch, don't be sad! We'll soon

find a nice home for you too,"
Louise comforted him, sitting
down on the floor and pulling
him onto her lap. Louise had a
way of stroking Patch in just the
right places – under his chin and
behind his ears and right on his
forehead above his nose – so that
he soon felt happy and purry
again. If only he could stay curled
up on Louise's lap for ever . . .

But just as he was thinking that,
Louise said, in a shaky voice,
"Some people are coming to look
for a kitten tonight so we've got
to have you looking your best."

She pulled a comb out of her
pocket. She looked like she was
trying hard not to cry. "I wish
you didn't have to go!"

Patch didn't want Louise to be sad. He knocked the comb out of her hand and jumped up onto her shoulder to rub his face against hers.

"Patch, stop it! Your whiskers really tickle!" Louise smiled, sounding braver as she reached up to grab him. "Come on. Let's get you ready! Dad says that Mr and Mrs Ferguson have got a nice big house with a huge garden. There'll be lots of trees for you to climb and loads of other cats around to play with. You're going to really like it!"

That evening Mr and Mrs Ferguson arrived at the cats' home in a red sports car which made a lot of noise as it pulled up. Louise went to the window to look at them as they walked up the front path. They were young and smartly dressed.

The man walked very quickly around all the cat runs, as though he was in a terrible rush.

"We haven't got much time," his wife, Clare, explained. "We have a dinner party to go to tonight.

Oh, look!" she exclaimed, stopping outside Patch's cage. "Isn't this one *so* cute?"

Patch did his best *not* to look cute by sticking his leg in the air and licking it the way he had seen the grown-up cats do. He always thought it made *them* look pretty silly.

"Look at the way he's cleaning himself! Isn't he sweet?" Clare said.

Patch stopped licking his leg and curled up in his box at the back of the run, with his back to them. Maybe if he showed them how sulky he could be they'd go away.

"Oh, how darling! He's such a shy little pudding!"

"Well, if he's too shy to get up to mischief then that'll suit us fine!" Clare's husband said, briskly. "We've just moved into a brand-new house, with all new furniture. In fact, he's the same colour as the living room carpet!"

Clare gave a silly giggle and said, "Here, pretty puss!" to Patch who made a face and started to scratch his ear. What he wouldn't give now for a good dose of fleas!

"The vet's checked him out. He's all ready to go," Louise's dad said.

"Fine. We'll go and fetch the cat basket from the car."

Louise was frowning as they hurried out. "You shouldn't pick a kitten just because it matches your carpet!" she said, angrily.

Her father smiled. "I expect they were just joking." He looked more serious as Louise's face looked sad. "Sweetheart, you know we can't keep Patch here."

"I never said that! I just don't want him to go somewhere where . . . where he'll get stepped on all the time because they can't tell the difference between him and their silly carpet!"

"Louise, now come on!" her father said, putting his arm round her. "You'll make Patch nervous if you act like this. Why don't you give him a chance to see if he likes his new home? Wouldn't that be best?"

So Louise gave Patch a final

cuddle and tried to pretend she was pleased for him as his new owners came back carrying their brand-new bright pink cat basket. "Be good, Patch!" she said, as she put him inside.

"Patch?" Clare said, curling up her nose when they got to the car. "Oh no, we'll give you a much more distinguished name than that, my precious!" She poked her long painted fingernails into Patch's basket and wiggled them about. "What about Humphrey?"

"But I *like* the name I have!" Patch miaowed, indignantly. Of course he didn't want to change it. Louise had given it to him. He miaowed that he wanted to be taken back to Louise immediately!

"He's got such a dear little miaow, hasn't he, darling?" Clare cooed. "He's just *so perfect*."

Patch stopped miaowing abruptly. What was it Oscar had said to him about his miaow? "You won't have to practise sounding pathetic when *you* want a saucer of milk! You have a naturally pathetic little mew! Some dotty old lady is going to spoil you rotten if you play your cards right!"

Patch didn't want to be spoilt by a dotty old lady – or a dotty *young* lady like the one who was calling him a cutie-pie as they drove away. He just wanted Louise.

Patch took a big breath and

filled his lungs with as much air
as possible. Then he gave the
loudest, most ear-piercing miaow
he had ever uttered in his life.
That was just for starters. By the
time Patch had miaowed as
loudly as he could for the whole

of the journey back, his new owners were raising their voices in order to hear each other.

"They'd better be right about him being house-trained!" Clare's husband shouted at her. "If not, we're taking him straight back!"

"House-trained? Of course I'm house-trained," Patch was about to tell them, when suddenly he had a much better idea!

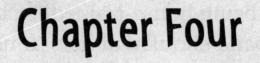

Chapter Four

Patch inspected the carpet in his
new home. It was true that he
blended in remarkably well with
it. It was multicoloured – a
mixture of brown and black and
orange and white – just like
Patch. And it had a nice feel to it
when Patch dug in his claws.

"Stop that, Humphrey!" Clare shrieked. "Here!" she said, plonking a scratching post down in front of Patch's nose. Patch immediately ran under the table.

The table had wooden legs like the one in Mrs Dodds's kitchen, but these legs were polished and had delicately carved feet at the bottom.

Patch decided to try his claws out on one of them. The wallpaper in this room looked quite promising too – not nearly as old and tatty as the stuff in Louise's kitchen – but it would do.

"HUMPHREY!" Clare screamed at him.

Patch ignored her. After all, *his* name wasn't Humphrey, was it?

His name was Patch!

"Patch!" Louise cried out, excitedly, the next day, as she spotted him back in his run when she got home from school. "What are you doing here?" Then she spotted her mother, who wasn't looking quite so pleased.

"Mr Ferguson brought him back this afternoon. He said they couldn't cope with his behaviour. I can't understand it. Patch was always such a perfect kitten when he was here with us."

"He still *is* perfect!" Louise said, opening the door of Patch's run and picking him up to cuddle him. Patch was purring loudly. "What did Patch do, Mum?" She

stroked Patch's head as she put
him down on the ground again.

"Apparently he acted like he'd
never seen a scratching post
before in his life," Louise's
mother sighed. "*Or* a litter tray!"

"Oh, dear." Louise frowned at
Patch, who was pretending to be
very interested in a piece of fluff

on the floor.

"Let's just hope someone else comes along soon," Mrs Dodds said. "Although I'm not sure the Fergusons were suited to a cat."

"Yes," said Louise, bravely. "Let's hope somebody really *nice* comes along soon."

But this time Patch really wasn't listening. He had spotted a spider and he was trying to tap it with his paw. By the time he had finished playing with it, Louise had gone away. Patch hoped she wasn't cross with him. He was just glad to be back near her again, that was all, and he wanted to tell her that. He knew she would come and see him again before she went to bed because she always did.

But that night she didn't. Louise's father came to check on him instead. "The sooner we get you out of here, the better, Patch," he said, gently, stroking him on his back.

"Where's Louise?" he miaowed, anxiously. Surely Louise wasn't so cross with him that she didn't love him any more? He felt so upset just thinking about it that he couldn't get to sleep. When he finally did, he had a horrible dream about Louise shouting at him and calling him a bad kitten.

"Oh, Patch!" Louise said, and for a moment Patch thought he was still dreaming until he opened his eyes and saw Louise

crouching down beside him
holding his bowl of breakfast.

Patch jumped up and rubbed
his head against her.

"Oh, Patch, I'm sorry I didn't
come and say goodnight last
night but Mum and Dad think
I'm getting too attached to you,"
Louise said. "Do you understand?
They think that the more time I

spend with you, the harder it's going to be for me to give you up again."

Patch didn't really understand. All he understood was that he felt happy again because Louise wasn't cross with him. And she was tickling him under his chin in just the way he liked best.

"Now, listen, Patch," Louise whispered. "There's a really nice old man called Mr Hedley coming to look for a kitten and Dad's already told him all about you. He sounds very kind and he wants a cat to stop him feeling lonely because he lives on his own."

Patch gave her a look that said, "Why can't I just stay here with you?" but either Louise didn't understand or she was pretending she didn't, to avoid having to give him an answer.

Later, when Mr Hedley came to take Patch home with him, Louise was nowhere in sight. Patch gave a little whimper as they put him inside a cosy box with a warm blanket. He sat very quietly the whole way home on the bus. The old man talked to him in a kind voice. He reassured him that he wouldn't be cross if Patch was naughty. But Patch didn't feel like he had the energy to be naughty. Besides, what good would it do? He'd never see Louise again anyway . . .

Chapter Five

Louise felt too sad to do anything after Patch left. She sat in her bedroom and ignored the telephone when it rang, even though she knew her mum and dad were both busy feeding the cats. But the phone kept ringing and when Louise's dad finally answered it, Louise's heart gave a little leap.

"Well, if that's the case, then of course you must bring him back," Mr Dodds was saying.

Is it Patch? Louise wondered, racing down the stairs as her dad hung up the phone. "Is Patch coming back again?"

Mr Dodds shook his head. "That was Mrs Smith. Her daughter wants her to go and live with her and she can't have a cat there. So she's bringing Oscar back tomorrow."

"Oh no, poor Oscar," Louise murmured. She had never felt as close to Oscar as she was to Patch. For one thing, she had always felt that Oscar didn't like her petting him and picking him up as much as Patch did. But she made up her mind to give him lots of affection to make up for losing his home with Mrs Smith.

Oscar arrived back looking very cross. Mrs Smith looked so sad as she gave him one last cuddle.

Oscar started miaowing loudly in protest.

"He'll settle down again after a while," Louise's dad said, and pretty soon Oscar did. At least, he stopped being noisy and went to sleep in his basket. In his dreams he was still lying on Mrs Smith's rug in front of the fire waiting for teatime, when he would have fresh boiled chicken and a saucer of milk all to himself.

When Oscar woke up Louise brought him some of his favourite chicken-flavoured cat food but he just sniffed at it and turned his head away.

"Oh, dear. We're both down in the dumps, aren't we?" Louise sighed. "You miss Mrs Smith and

I miss Patch. Let's just hope that Patch isn't feeling as sad as we are."

Two days later, Louise was upstairs doing her homework, when the doorbell rang. She heard her mum go to answer it. Then she heard a voice she recognised, so she ran downstairs to see what was happening.

Mr Hedley was standing in their hallway carrying a large cardboard box.

"He hasn't been naughty," Mr Hedley was saying as he handed the box to Louise's mum. "He's just been so sad that I couldn't bear it any longer. He hasn't eaten anything. I couldn't even tempt him with some fresh chicken."

Louise rushed over to the box and cried out, "Patch!"

A loud miaow answered her. A few moments later Louise was holding Patch in her arms and he was purring frantically as he rubbed his head against her chest.

"Oh, so you *can* purr!" Mr Hedley said, smiling.

Mrs Dodds was shaking her head in disbelief as she watched the fuss Patch and Louise were making of each other.

"It seems that Patch has already found his perfect owner!" Mr Hedley added, his eyes twinkling as he looked on. He glanced mischievously at Louise's mum. "Don't you agree, Mrs Dodds?"

Chapter Six

Louise couldn't stop smiling after her mum finally agreed that she could keep Patch.

Mr Hedley was smiling too but he sounded a bit sad as he stroked Patch goodbye and said, "I expect I'm too old to think about giving a home to a lively young kitten."

Suddenly Louise had an idea. She looked at her mum.

Louise led the way to Oscar's run, where he was lying curled up with his back to them, pretending to be asleep.

"Oscar!" Patch cried out, excitedly, and when Louise opened the door of the run he leaped out of her arms and scampered over to tell Oscar that he was back – and for good!

But Oscar, who was in a very bad mood indeed, snarled, "Leave me alone!"

"Someone's feeling sorry for himself, eh, Puss?" a kind, elderly voice said.

Oscar hid his face under one

paw, rudely.

Patch started to describe how
old Mr Hedley had a log fire and
had tried to tempt him with fresh
chicken and chopped liver and a
saucer of egg yolk.

"Egg yolk?" Oscar sniffed.
"Liver?" His mouth was
beginning to water.

"That's right!" Patch said.

"Oscar isn't himself at all since he had to leave Mrs Smith's," Mrs Dodds was explaining. "Normally he's much more mischievous than this." She smiled. "Although he thinks we don't know that."

"Mischievous, eh?" Mr Hedley was reaching down to stroke him. "Well, that sounds just right for me. I like mischievous kittens."

Oscar sniffed the old man's hands. He liked the smell of them. He stood up and licked them. They tasted good too, almost as good as old Mrs Smith's after she'd been chopping up chicken for him.

Oscar suddenly felt very hungry. He felt so hungry he

reckoned he could eat a whole
chicken! He decided that Mr
Hedley might make a good
owner after a bit of training and
he rubbed his head against him to
tell him that. He also wanted to
let Patch know that Mr Hedley
was *his* property now!

"Well, it looks like we've got two perfect kittens belonging to two perfect owners," Mrs Dodds laughed.

Both Patch and Oscar disagreed. *They* thought it was more a case of two perfect owners belonging to two perfect kittens, but they didn't say anything. It was just too difficult to purr and talk at the same time!

Collect all of JENNY DALE'S KITTEN TALES!

The prices shown below are correct at the time of going to press. However, Macmillan Publishers reserve the right to show new retail prices on covers which may differ from those previously advertised.

MORE KITTEN TALES BOOKS FOLLOW SOON!

All Macmillan titles can be ordered at your local bookshop or are available by post from:

Book Service by Post
PO Box 29, Douglas, Isle of Man IM99 1BQ

Credit cards accepted. For details:
Telephone: 01624 675137
Fax: 01624 670923
E-mail: bookshop@enterprise.net

Free postage and packing in the UK.
Overseas customers: add £1 per book (paperback)
and £3 per book (hardback).